D0851728

The Washout

H 10 9 8 7 6 5 4
Text copyright © 1978 by Carol Carrick
Illustrations copyright © 1978 by Donald Carrick
All rights reserved. No part of this book may be reproduced or transmitted in any form or by any means, electronic or mechanical, including photocopying, recording or by any information storage and retrieval system, without permission in writing from the publisher.

Library of Congress Cataloging in Publication Data
Carrick, Carol. The Washout.
Summary: When a summer storm washes out the road. Christopher decides to row around the lake for help—and almost gets into serious trouble.
[1. Storms—Fiction] I. Carrick, Donald. II Title.
PZ7.C2344Was [E] 78-1835 ISBN 0-395-28781-2 PA ISBN 0-89919-850-3

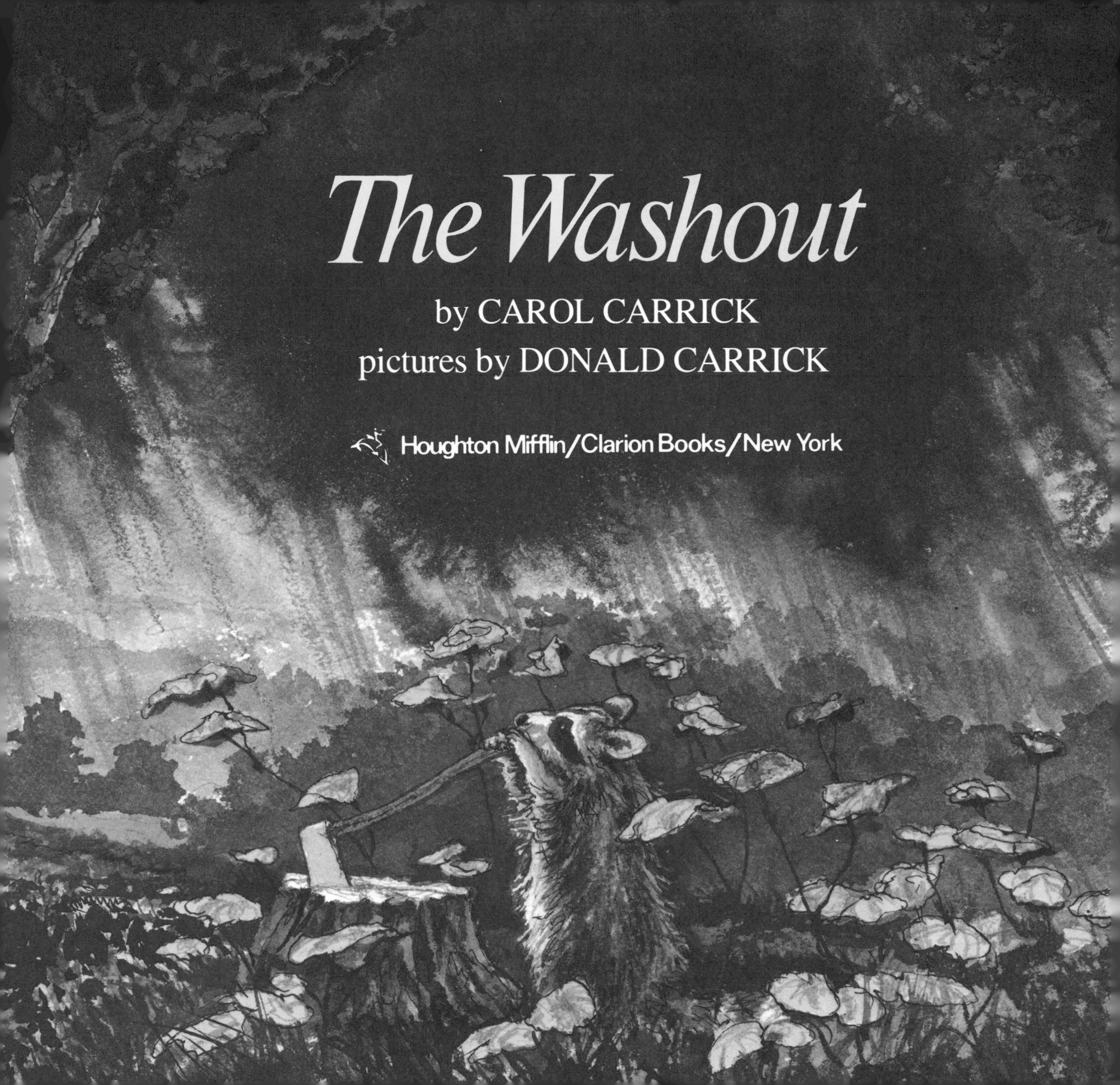

The Washout

by CAROL CARRICK

pictures by DONALD CARRICK

Houghton Mifflin/Clarion Books/New York

The minute Christopher opened his eyes that morning, he knew something had happened. His room was filled with a dim, wavering light as if he were underwater. At the window was a wall of leaves. He hadn't heard the tree crash down in the storm, just missing the house.

Christopher and his mother had arrived at their summer cottage just after dinner the night before. His father was coming on the train next weekend when his vacation started.

"Mom!" Christopher called. "A tree blew over right outside my window."

"There are trees down all around the house," his mother answered. "One must have hit the power line. We have no electricity and the telephone isn't working either."

Christopher was excited. He hoped they wouldn't have to drive back home. "We can stay, can't we?" he asked.

"Sure," his mother replied. "The power should be back on in a little while. As soon as you get dressed, we'll drive down to the general store and stock up on some groceries. We can use the phone there."

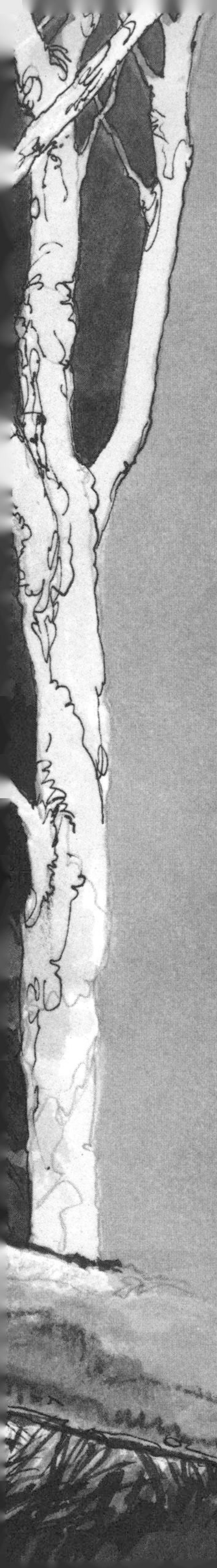

They drove a short way and then stopped. Their road had washed out.

"Oh, no!" his mother groaned. "What more can possibly go wrong?"

They got out of the car and stood looking down into the ditch across the road. It was twice as wide and maybe as deep as Christopher was tall.

"I could get across," Christopher said. "And then I could hike down to the store for you. Really!"

His mother shook her head. "We'd better wait till the water is lower. Just look at it."

In dry times the little brook that ran under their dirt road was only a clear trickle. Now its muddy water had caved in the road and swept it downhill through the forest.

"Let's go back to the house," his mother said. "We'll have to wait until we can call the road crew."

But Christopher wanted to explore. "Aw, please, Mom," he begged. "I won't be long."

"Well, all right," she said as she started the car. "But I can't help worrying. Don't go near any fallen wires. And stay out of the brook. It's moving too fast."

As soon as his mother started to back up, Christopher slid down the embankment, hanging on to saplings. His dog, Ben, took off in another direction, following the new sounds and smells of his first summer in the country.

Christopher looked for the log or the large rocks he always used to cross the brook. The log was still there but it had trapped a lot of branches and stones, and now the brook spilled over it like a waterfall. He followed the stream all the way to the lake without ever finding the rock bridge.

The lake had flooded over their beach. Christopher heard a gentle thunk, thunk. Somebody's boat had broken loose from its mooring and was bumping against the trees. Maybe he could row across the lake and hitch a ride to the general store.

A soggy milk carton to bail out the rainwater was floating in the boat. Christopher found it was slow work. Ben had lost interest in the woods and joined him in a game of dodge the bailing water.

There were no oars. Christopher found a dead young tree and pulled with all his weight until it snapped. He climbed into the boat and pushed off.

He soon got the hang of keeping his balance standing in the boat, but he had forgotten that the lake was too deep to pole across. The wind was against him and the current brought him back to shore.

Then he got the idea of poling the boat along the shore till he reached the other side of the lake. One good push sent him drifting quite a way.

Ben followed along the shore until he came to a place where the underbrush was thick. After that, Christopher could hear him crashing through the woods. The only bothersome thing was the black flies hovering in the shade. Christopher had worked up a sweat and the tiny insects tormented him and stuck in his eyes. He took off his jacket and hung it over his head.

Christopher was now pushing against a wall of rock, the base of the tall cliffs. This was his favorite place when he and his dad went canoeing. He liked to imagine Indians watching them from the top.

There was a splash. Christopher looked back. He had never seen Ben swim before. The dog looked funny paddling after the boat, his paws churning and his tail streaming out behind. Then it seemed like too much of an effort for him to keep up. Ben was puffing hard. But he wouldn't be able to climb out of the water till they got past the cliffs.

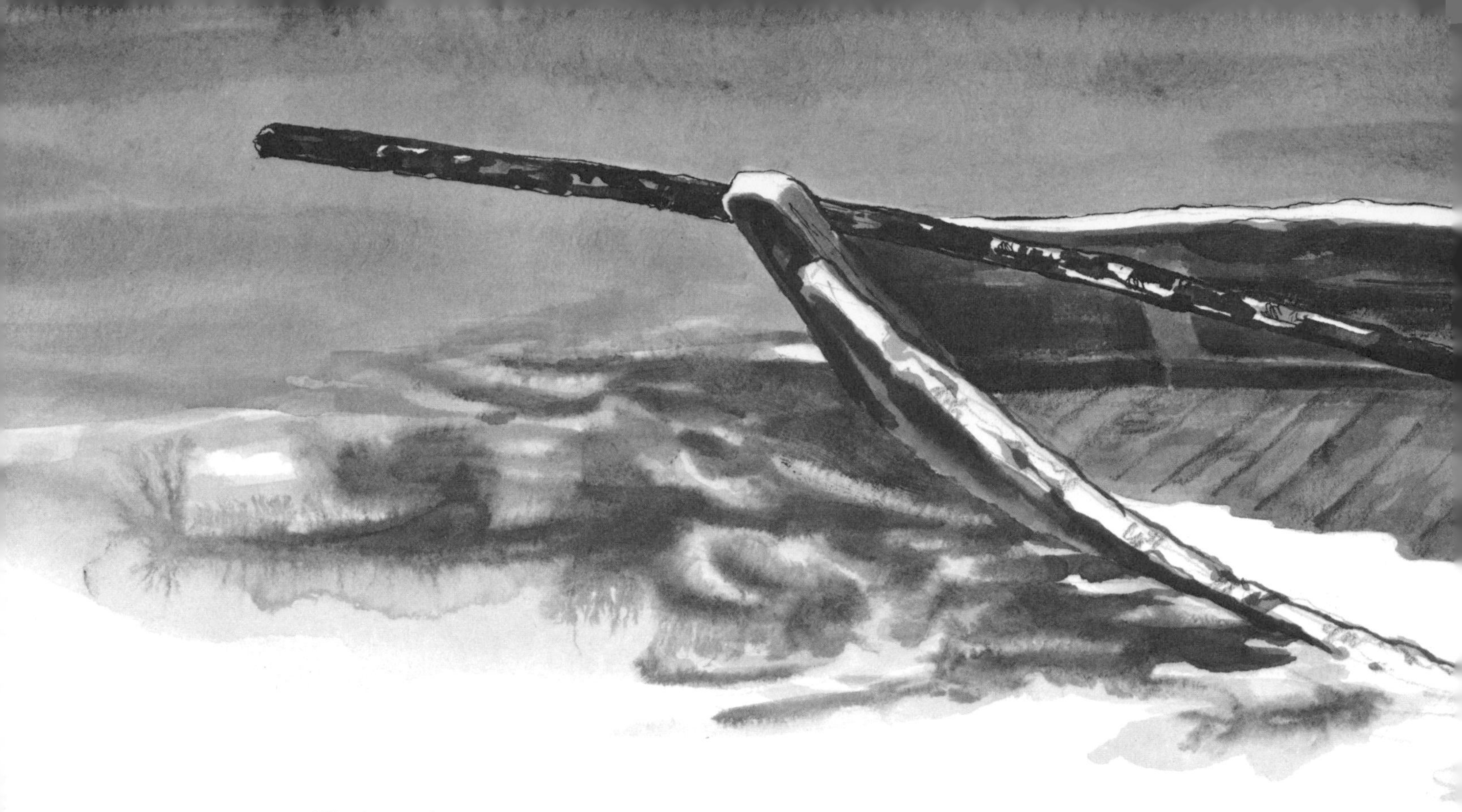

Christopher called Ben to the side of the boat and tried to pull him in. But the struggling dog was heavy. When the boat tipped way over, more water started coming in. Christopher lost his balance and almost fell overboard.

His heart was pounding. He realized he was alone on the lake and how close he had come to falling in. The water was deep here. Some said no one had ever found bottom.

He felt hungry without any breakfast and wished he was home. Still, he couldn't go back the way he had come. He would have to pole against the current all the way and then climb uphill to their house. It would take forever.

He poled along, anxiously watching Ben and calling words of encouragement. At last they came to the end of the cliffs. But Ben continued to swim. He was enjoying it . . . a regular water dog!

After Christopher rounded the lake he pulled the boat as high up on shore as he could. It was only a short walk to the road, but the ground was mushy. The mud sucked at him like quicksand, and as Christopher pulled each foot free, he was afraid of losing his boots.

When he reached the road, Christopher took off his belt and looped it through Ben's collar. Ben wasn't used to walking on a leash. He had to be pulled most of the way. But Christopher was afraid to let Ben run loose on the road.

Christopher's socks had gotten wet and his boots rubbed. He took them off. His feet were tender. He hadn't walked barefoot since last summer. He tried to get a ride, but the few cars that came along drove right past. No one wanted to pick up a wet boy with a muddy dog.

At last he saw Humphrey's store ahead. Even though he was tired, Christopher began to trot. Ben was tired, too, but he thought this was another game and ran ahead.

Mr. Humphrey was talking to some other men about the storm. When he noticed Christopher he said, "Why Christopher, have you come up already? Summer must be here."

Christopher told him that their road had washed out and they had no food or electricity. The men were impressed with Christopher's story about how he had gotten there, but they agreed that his mother would be very worried by now.

Mr. Humphrey said, "We'll get Ed, here, to take you home. Tell your mother that I'll let the state trooper and the road crew know you're up there."

He filled two bags with food and then looked at Christopher over his glasses and added two cherry tarts. "Just in case you're out of cherry tarts," he said.

CANDY

Ed's truck lurched and skidded up the rutted hill to Christopher's house until they came to a fallen tree that blocked the road. The tree was too heavy for both of them to lift, so Ed took the chain saw from the floor of the truck and cut it up.

As they came over the hill, Christopher saw his mother waiting in the road. When they got out of the truck she said, "I heard the chain saw. Christopher, where have you been all this time?"

"To Humphrey's store," he answered, as if he did it every day. "Look what I got." He held up one of the bags.

The water level in the ditch had dropped since morning. Ed climbed down to help Christopher and Ben scramble across.

His mother kneeled and put her hands on Christopher's shoulders. He could see that she had been crying. "You knew that I would be worried when you were gone so long," she said. "I was afraid something had happened to you."

Christopher looked down at his feet. He hadn't meant to upset her. "I know, Mom. I'm sorry." Still, he couldn't help being proud of what he had done. "But aren't you glad I did it?" he asked.

His mother waved as Ed gave a good-by toot and then she looked at the bags from Humphrey's store.

"Yes, I'm glad, Christopher." She laughed. "Now let's eat. I'm starved!"